O Christmas Tree

O CHRISTMAS TREE

by Vashanti Rahaman
Pictures by Frané Lessac

Boyds Mills Press

Text copyright © 1996 by Vashanti Rahaman
Illustrations copyright © 1996 by Frané Lessac

Published by Caroline House
Boyds Mills Press, Inc.
A Highlights Company
815 Church Street
Honesdale, Pennsylvania 18431
Printed in China

Publisher Cataloging-in-Publication Data
Rahaman, Vashanti.
    O Christmas tree / by Vashanti Rahaman ; paintings by Frané Lessac.—1st ed.
[32]p. : col. ill. ; cm.
Summary : A boy wants an evergreen tree for Christmas in this story set in the West Indies.
ISBN 1-56397-237-9
1. Christmas trees—Fiction—Juvenile literature. 2. Christmas—Juvenile fiction.
[1. Christmas trees—Fiction. 2. Christmas—Fiction.] I. Lessac, Frané, ill. II. Title.
    [E]—dc20   1996   AC   CIP
Library of Congress Catalog Card Number 95-83193

First edition, 1996
Book designed by Tim Gillner
The text of this book is set in 14-point Stone Serif.
The illustrations are done in gouache.

10 9 8 7 6 5 4 3

*To my parents and brothers and the
Christmas memories we share*

—V. R.

For Nicholas and Ali, with warm regards

—F. L.

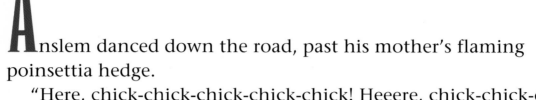

Anslem danced down the road, past his mother's flaming poinsettia hedge.

"Here, chick-chick-chick-chick-chick! Heeere, chick-chick-chick-chick-chick!" Miss Mary, who lived on the other side of the hedge, was feeding her fowls.

"Morning, Miss Mary," Anslem called. "I going and watch them unload the Christmas boat. Pa say we could get a real Christmas tree this year."

"Huh!" said Miss Mary, scattering a handful of fowl food. "Why real have to come in boat from away? It have real here, too."

"But real Christmas trees don't grow here," said Anslem.

"Is all right, child," said Miss Mary. "Go and watch your boat."

By the time Anslem reached the docks, the Caribbean sun had already warmed the day. Scents of salt and fish and motor oil swirled pungently together. And the little "slap-slap" sounds of the waves were drowned out by roaring motors, rattling chains, and shouting workers. On top of all that, transistor radios blared out Christmas carols and calypso.

Anslem sat on a cable spool and watched the swarm of little boats bringing cargo from the big ship. He watched cranes unloading Christmas things that came to the West Indies from abroad. He watched big trucks coming and going. He watched for the Christmas trees.

Day was nearly done when the first load of Christmas trees reached shore. Anslem didn't know whether to hold his head and bawl, or to hold his belly and laugh. Must be a bad joke, he thought.

But it was no joke. The growing pile of trees on the jetty was real—a real pile of dry bush.

In other years, the trees had arrived looking fresh and green. But this year, the first year Anslem's family could afford a Christmas tree, they had arrived looking like rubbish. They were so dry that not a single tree had a single needle on it.

Anslem was too vexed and too disappointed to even bawl. He turned his back on the dead trees and headed home.

Downtown was decorated for Christmas. Anslem passed fake Santas in shop windows. He passed fake trees covered with fake snow. Fake, he thought as he trudged on by, fake just like Christmas down here. All this thing we does sing about in Christmas carol, I never hope to see that. All this fireplace and sled and snowman on Christmas card, I never hope to see that. All I was hoping for was a real Christmas tree, just one time, to touch it and smell it and get a feel and a smell of real Christmas.

Anslem sniffed and swallowed his tears. Surprised, he sniffed again. There was no mistaking that sweet, smoky, Christmas smell. Must be Miss Mary, he thought.

Sure enough, Miss Mary had her Christmas ham boiling in a big tin on a fire in the yard. She was busy fanning the flames.

Anslem's mother had been busy, too. On the front porch were two gallon bottles, one filled with pink sorrel drink, and the other filled with clear ginger beer.

As Anslem lifted the latch on the porch gate, his Ma called, "Anslem, bring the sorrel and the ginger inside, boy."

Anslem carefully picked up the glass bottles. Once Ma started making ginger and sorrel you knew Christmas was near. Next, she would take a whole day to make black cake with the raisins and currants soaking in the big jar.

But as soon as Anslem pushed open the front door with his foot, he knew that Ma had already finished making the black cake. Only black cake, full of molasses and butter and raisins and spice, could make a house smell like that.

Anslem's mouth watered as he counted the cakes.

"Leave my cake and wash your hand," said Ma. "Your pa will reach home for supper just now."

"So what you did today, boy?" asked Pa when his plate was empty.

Anslem told about the trees. "And it's not fair," he said, blinking and blinking to dry his eyes. "Not fair to bring dead trees."

"Boy," said Pa, getting up from the table, "not fair is when hurricane pass and take everything you work for. Nothing like that happen now. It don't take tree to make Christmas."

"Yes, Pa," said Anslem.

Ma squeezed Pa's hand. Then she got up, too, and kissed Anslem on his forehead. "Come help your ma clean the kitchen," she said.

The next day Anslem went back to the docks and asked for a dried-up tree.

"Take what you want," said one of the dock workers. "Those trees are only good to throw away."

So Anslem set out for home with two of the biggest trees he could find. There is some gravel left from the new house by Miss Mary's neighbor, he thought, as he dragged the trees through town. And Ma has an old bucket with a hole. And Pa has a half tin of old white paint from when the house used to be white.

All that will work, he thought, as he and the trees took a rest by the roadside.

When he finally got home, Anslem set to work.

Hours later, tired and dirty and spattered with paint, he called Pa and Ma into the backyard.

Ma stared at the two naked trees standing in a bucket of gravel and shook her head.

"It look just like the expensive artificial tree in the shop, not so, Ma?" said Anslem.

White paint covered the trees and the gravel and the bucket and half of the backyard.

"Like you was trying for a white Christmas," said Pa. "What's that smell?"

"I spray it with pine cleaner so it would smell like a real tree," said Anslem. "I did a good job, eh?"

Ma threw her apron over her head and started making funny noises. Anslem couldn't tell if she was laughing or crying.

Pa pushed his cap back on his head and gave Anslem a big hug. "You did good, child," he said, "maybe too good."

"What you mean, Pa?" said Anslem.

"I mean," said Pa, "it have no way at all that your tree going and fit in the house."

As Anslem was thinking that over, a strong breeze blew through the yard. Anslem's arrangement trembled. The two trees yawned apart. Then the whole contraption capsized, trees and gravel and bucket and all.

"Ah-ah-ah! What trouble is this?" said Ma.

"Christmas fall down, is what," said Anslem, wiping away his tears. "Sorry, Ma. Let me clean up the mess."

"Don't worry, son," said Pa. "Go take a bath. Your ma will make some tea for you. It going and take my big cutlass to chop that tree, and you can't handle that."

Maybe, thought Anslem, as he scrubbed and scrubbed at the paint all over him; maybe Christmas is plenty, plenty little things—little things like how Ma and Pa take that big mess out there so easy.

On Christmas day, right after the early-morning church service, Miss Mary brought over some of her ham and stayed for breakfast. She inspected the colored lights by the windows. She examined the Christmas cards on the walls. "But what happen about the Christmas tree you was going and get?" she asked Anslem.

"A big nothing happen," he said. "I just find out it have more to Christmas than Christmas tree."

Miss Mary pulled Anslem into a hug that smelled strongly of English lavender. "You really think that is a big nothing, child?" she asked.

"No," said Anslem, trying to wriggle out, "that is a special, special something. But a Christmas tree would still be nice."

"Nice is how you see it, child," said Miss Mary, as she pinched his chin gently and let him go. "Nice could be right in front you, but you busy looking behind."

"If nice was there, I would have seen it," said Anslem.

"Think about it, child," said Miss Mary.

Anslem leaned out the window to watch the Christmas sunrise.

And then he saw them—Christmas trees—real, live Christmas trees. Miss Mary was right. They had been there all the time.

"Look!" he shouted, dancing around. "The poinsettia! The poinsettia! Them is Christmas tree for true!"

"For true," said Miss Mary, with a knowing smile. "For true!"

Author's Note

Christmas first came to the Caribbean with people from Europe who ruled the islands for a long time. So, many of the Christmas traditions I grew up with were really European. They often had more to do with winter than with Christmas. But West Indians do not give up traditions easily—even traditions like Christmas trees and carols about snow that seem a little out of place on tropical islands.

Adopting traditions from other places is another West Indian tradition. Our ancestors came from places like Africa, Europe, Asia, and the Middle East. This collection of cultures has resulted in a unique mix of traditions on each island. While people from West Africa were taken to all of the Caribbean countries, people from India settled in only a few places in the region. The English colonized some islands while the French, Spanish, Dutch, and Danish colonized others. So different islands have slightly different traditions.

O Christmas Tree takes place on an island that used to belong to England, rather like the one where I grew up. The people in the story speak English with a West Indian flair, and sometimes slip from dialect to standard English and back, like I do.

The black cake that Anslem's mother makes is our favorite cake for Christmas and weddings and other special occasions. It is probably a version of the dark fruitcakes and plum puddings that are popular in England. But in true West Indian style, not all of our Christmas traditions come from England or other parts of Europe. The ginger drink mentioned in the story is a festive tradition from West Africa. We make it by soaking fresh ginger in water for a few days, then sweeten it with sugar. To make a sorrel drink, we use a relative of the hibiscus flower instead of ginger.

As for the poinsettia growing in West Indian gardens, we know that Christmas is near when it turns red. But the poinsettia is a plant from Mexico. Like the Christmas trees, the carols about snow, the black cake, and the ginger drink, poinsettias are a Christmas tradition that West Indians have adopted. And like those other adopted traditions, they have become a part of Christmas in the West Indies forever.